Suddenly, he noticed the piano.

It was not as tall a dropping-off place as he would have liked, but it would have to do for now. He held tight to his egg package and stepped up on the piano stool. Before he knew it he was lying on his stomach on top of the upright piano. Unfortunately, his nose began to tickle, probably because of the feathers.

Paul held his breath, inched closer to the edge of the and counted to ten. All at once he let go and his e fell. There was a sickening wet, crunching g package hit the floor.

ked wet and yucky.

Books by Janice Harrell

The Great Egg Bust
Tiffany, the Disaster

Available from MINSTREL Books

THE GREAT EGG BUST

Janice Harrell

A MINSTREL® BOOK

PUBLISHED BY POCKET BOOKS

New York   London   Toronto   Sydney   Tokyo   Singapore

A MINSTREL PAPERBACK *ORIGINAL*

A Minstrel Book published by
POCKET BOOKS, a division of Simon & Schuster Inc.
1230 Avenue of the Americas, New York, NY 10020

Copyright © 1993 by Janice Harrell
Illustrations Copyright © 1992 by Lucy Montgomery

ISBN: 0-671-72861-X

First Minstrel Books printing May 1993

10 9 8 7 6 5 4 3 2 1

A MINSTREL BOOK and colophon are registered trademarks
of Simon & Schuster Inc.

Cover art by Lina Levy

Printed in the U.S.A.

Chapter
One

I hate Tiffany Bonner," said Paul.

"Why, Paul," said his mother. "I thought you liked Tiffany."

"No," said Paul firmly.

"You worried about her, anyway. When she moved away, you wrote her a letter, remember?"

Paul remembered, but it had all happened so long ago. Last year, when he was in the third grade, Tiffany had lived with a family in Paul's neighborhood. But when it hadn't worked out, she moved away and had been adopted by a completely different family. All of a sudden Paul's world had seemed unsteady. He was adopted, too, and people shouldn't move from one family to another, in his opinion. It would have worried anybody. But all that was last year and felt like ancient history.

"I don't care," he said stubbornly. "Tiffany is a pain. She has *always* been a pain."

"It hasn't been easy for Tiffany living with so many different foster families." Mrs. Fenner grated some cheese onto a cutting board. "She's getting along very well now that she's been adopted by the Bonners, but you should try to understand that she might still feel insecure."

Paul's mother was a social worker. She was always making excuses for people. He was used to it.

"Anyway, Paul, now that Tiffany has moved away, when do you ever even see her?"

"Everywhere!" cried Paul. "She's all over the place."

Mrs. Fenner smiled as she scraped the cheese into a bowl. "I think you're exaggerating."

Paul wasn't exaggerating. Now that Paul went for swimming at the YMCA after school, he saw Tiffany there almost every day.

"You know what Tiffany is?" Paul asked. "She's a bleep."

"A *what?*"

"A bleep." Paul smiled. He had seen movies on TV on the Family Channel. Whenever a character got really angry, his mouth would open but nothing would come out. Paul's parents said the channel had "bleeped" a bad word. Paul could usually figure out for himself what word they had cut.

Paul's mother grinned. "She's a bleep, huh? Now I've heard it all."

2

Paul's mother didn't know the half of it. If she had been at the swimming lessons at the Y, she would have seen just how much of a bleep Tiffany was.

When Paul first started going to the YMCA for swimming after school, he had liked it a lot. A van picked up kids from Paul's school and drove them to the YMCA. That way Paul got to swim every day. When he got out of the pool, he sat in the lounge and drew or did homework until his father picked him up after work. It was a pretty neat setup until the day Tiffany walked in.

Paul stared at her. "What are you doing here?"

She sat down on the sofa next to him. Unfortunately, she was not a bit shy. "I come to swimming lessons here," she said.

"I thought you were just learning." Paul remembered seeing her at the beginner's classes.

"I'm coming along by leaps and bounds," she said. "Mrs. Horowitz says I'll be a terrific swimmer some day."

"You've got a long way to go." Paul was a good swimmer. Not that he went around bragging about it the way Tiffany would have done. But during the summer he had learned how to jump in the pool fully clothed, strip off his jeans, and tie them into a makeshift float. He had always been interested in survival techniques.

Nobody Paul knew swam as well as he did. He not only swam better than his friends, Suzy Hart and Billy Blakely, he even swam better than his mother. He hated to think that Tiffany was catching up with him, coming along by "leaps and bounds."

"Mrs. Horowitz says most of the best swimmers are big," said Tiffany, "because they can reach a long way and kick hard. How tall are you? I'm four feet nine inches."

Paul was four feet five inches when he stood on his tiptoes. Gloomily he decided he was probably going to grow up to be a midget. "I can't keep up with how tall I am," he said loudly. "I'm growing all the time."

Tiffany gazed at him steadily, as if she were measuring herself against him. "At my new school I have to take my reading with the fifth grade," she said.

Paul did not say anything. Reading had never been particularly easy for him. He liked arithmetic better. But what he liked even less than reading, he decided, was Tiffany. It was just not fair that Tiffany could read so well and that she got to be tall on top of it.

"I'm the *only* kid in the fourth grade who gets to go to the fifth grade for reading," Tiffany went on proudly.

"I got it when you said it the first time, Tiffany," said Paul. "You don't have to explain."

"My school has flowers outside," Tiffany said, "and my teacher, Miss Burack, is pretty and nice, and the water in the water fountains is ice-cold."

Paul rolled his eyes. He was sure now that she was making it all up. Who ever heard of a school where the water in the fountains was ice-cold?

"Women make the best long-distance swimmers," said Tiffany. "They have better endurance, Mrs. Horowitz says. They have more body fat, too, and that's good for long-distance swimming."

Paul wished Tiffany would go into long-distance swimming. She could swim all the way to the other side of the world, for all he cared. As for Mrs. Horowitz, he wished she would go soak her head in the deep end of the pool.

Having Tiffany bugging him was one of the things Paul had decided he did not like about being in the fourth grade. The other thing he didn't like was the homework.

"One hour and twenty-five minutes," Paul told his mother while she cooked dinner one night. "That's how long it took me to do my dumb homework."

"Are you counting the time you spent talking to Billy on the phone?"

6

"I only talked to Billy for a minute. Don't you believe me, Mom? I'm telling you, Mrs. Hux gives us too much homework."

"Of course I believe you, Paul. But I guess you've got to expect more homework now that you're in the fourth grade."

"It's not fair."

When the family sat down at the table for supper, Paul tried a different approach.

"The stuff Mrs. Hux gives us is really boring," Paul told his dad. "It's the same stuff over and over again. And I already know it all, anyway."

"What would make it more interesting, do you think?" asked Mr. Fenner.

"No homework!" cried Paul.

His father smiled. "I'm not sure we can arrange that, Paul."

"It's just that it's so stupid," said Paul. "You should see it. The same stuff over and over."

"That's because not everybody catches on as fast as you, sport." Mr. Fenner rumpled Paul's hair.

"Perhaps we could talk to Mrs. Hux," said Paul's mom. "Maybe she could give you some extra work that would be more challenging."

Paul looked at her, horrified. She hadn't caught on at all. More homework wasn't what he needed. He needed *less* homework. "Wait a minute," he

7

said. "I've got too much work already. That's the whole problem."

"Maybe something could be worked out so that the kids who score over a certain amount on a quiz could skip doing the homework and do something else instead," Mrs. Fenner suggested.

"It's an idea," said Mr. Fenner.

Paul could almost taste his victory over Mrs. Hux. Mrs. Hux was tough, and ordinarily Paul would not have figured there was much chance of getting her to cut down on the homework. But his mother the social worker was used to dealing with tough cases. Mrs. Hux would be a piece of cake to her. And Paul's father would be sure to back her up. Mr. Fenner taught in the local college and was always reading out loud from editorials in the paper that said elementary education was in terrible shape. Paul figured that Mrs. Hux would have to listen when his parents complained.

If his parents succeeded in cutting the homework, his life would be practically perfect. Then he was struck by a sudden thought—it would be perfect, that is, if he could only get Tiffany to quit bugging him.

Chapter
Two

"Did you talk to Mrs. Hux?" Paul asked his parents after they got back from Parents' Night.

"Yes." Mrs. Fenner tossed her purse onto the couch. "We talked to her."

"So, what is she going to do?"

"We discussed several possibilities." Paul's father smiled.

Paul knew that his father would never smile like that just because of getting Mrs. H. to cut down on homework. Paul gave him a look. "Don't forget that the idea is to cut the homework. It's not going to do me any good if I just get a bunch of a different *kind* of homework."

"Gotcha, kiddo." Mr. Fenner rumpled Paul's hair. "We're working on it. I promise."

Paul began keeping a chart of how much time it took him to do his homework. He got a piece of graph paper, which had hundreds of tiny squares on it. For every five minutes he spent on his homework, he neatly filled in a square with his pencil.

"See?" he said to his parents after he had been keeping track of the homework for two weeks. "I'm not making it up. I spend all my time doing homework, practically. I don't have time to do anything that's really"—he tried to think of a word that would appeal to his father—"educational," he finished triumphantly. "Like my stamp collection or my rock collection or my trumpet practice."

Mr. Fenner put on his glasses and looked at Paul's graph. "This is very good, Paul."

"The only thing is," said Mrs. Fenner, "I wonder if you aren't spending more time filling in those little boxes on the graph than you're spending on your homework."

"Mom!" protested Paul. "Stop it!"

"Hang on, Paul," said Mr. Fenner. "Just hang in there. Help is on the way."

Paul wished that Tiffany were the kind of problem that could be solved by his parents working on it. Paul couldn't even *imagine* any solution to his problem with Tiffany.

After swim class Tiffany came into the lounge, where Paul was watching cartoons, and sat down on the couch next to him. "Get lost!" Paul said. "Go sit somewhere else."

"I can sit anywhere I want." Tiffany opened her notebook on her lap.

The coach walked by them on his way back from the snack bar.

"Coach!" cried Tiffany.

"Be quiet, Tiffany." Paul frowned. "Go ahead and sit here. See if I care." He got up and moved to the green plastic chair by the television.

"I like my new school a lot better than my old school," Tiffany said. "It's a better school. Everybody says so. We always win at everything."

"You're full of it," said Paul.

"Coach!" cried Tiffany.

Luckily Coach Harper didn't hear her. His tennis shoes made squeaking sounds on the floor as he turned and disappeared into the hallway to the locker rooms.

On television Ranger Bob was showing drawings. They were mostly by little kids. Lots were of rainbows. Square houses with chimneys and curly smoke were another popular subject. Paul was sure he drew much more interesting pictures than that.

"And now for the birthdays!" Ranger Bob cried. A long list, the names of the birthday kids, began rolling over the television screen.

11

After "Happy Birthday" was finished playing, Ranger Bob gave the address for sending in birthdays and drawings. Paul wrote it down on the back of the picture he was drawing. He thought maybe he would send the picture in. He had just drawn a sea serpent whose big snout curled up out of the sea in an impressive sneer. Pointed fins like triangles were lined up along the sea serpent's back.

Paul glanced over at Tiffany and frowned. "You're copying my picture!"

"I am not."

Paul turned over his drawing so she could not see it.

"What's yours?" asked Tiffany as she filled in the triangular fins on her picture with pink crayon.

"It's a sea serpent."

"Mine's a mermaid," said Tiffany.

"Mermaids don't have fins," said Paul. "They have tails."

"How do you know?" asked Tiffany. "Have you ever seen a mermaid?"

A car horn beeped. Paul quickly grabbed his books and notebooks and ran to the door.

"Boy, am I glad to see you," he told his father as he slid into the front seat.

"Am I late?" asked Mr. Fenner, glancing at his watch. "I thought I was early."

Paul sighed. "It's that Tiffany. She keeps bugging me."

Tiffany had her nose pressed against the glass door. Mr. Fenner waved to her and then drove away.

"Don't let her get to you, Paul. Just remember she's had a tough life."

Paul was tired of hearing about how Tiffany had had a tough life. Did that give her the right to bug him forever?

"I talked to your teacher this afternoon," Mr. Fenner said. "It's all set. We're going to have a city-wide Science Olympiad for fourth graders." He looked pleased. "Sort of like the real Olympics, but instead of athletics, this competition will be in brains."

"It sounds kind of like homework," said Paul suspiciously.

"No! It's not a bit like homework. There'll be a contest to see who can build the best container to keep an egg from breaking and another contest to see who can build a toy car that will go farthest using only the power of a mousetrap. Our plan is to encourage teamwork and to promote an interest in science."

"I don't know," said Paul, getting interested. "How is that going to help me with all my homework?"

13

"Here's the kicker," crowed Mr. Fenner. "Kids who participate will be exempt from certain homework as long as they keep a B average on the quizzes."

"Sounds good." Paul grinned. He couldn't wait to tell Billy.

Chapter
Three

At lunch the next day Paul tried to explain to Billy about the Science Olympiad. "It's like a contest," Paul said. "It would be more fun if we both enter. And remember, if we do, we won't have to do all that homework."

Billy stirred chocolate milk into his mashed potatoes. He was always doing disgusting things with his food. One time Mrs. Hux had made him eat the food he had mixed together, but it hadn't discouraged him a bit. "I don't know. I'm already pretty busy, particularly since I got my Nintendo."

"But if you do this contest and you keep a B average on your quizzes, you'll have all kinds of free time to play Nintendo. No homework, man! Do you hear what I'm saying?"

"Yeah." Billy poured raisins onto the mashed potatoes and pressed them in with a spoon. "But if I don't make B's on the quizzes, then I'd still have to do the homework."

"Oh, come on!" said Paul. "It'll be fun."

Billy popped a cracker into his mouth as he thought about it. Finally he said, "Well, okay. Maybe I'll give it a try. But only if you promise you'll help me."

Paul's smile grew. Even if he ended up doing a lot of the work for Billy, he wouldn't mind. It would be worth it if he didn't have to do that dumb homework.

That afternoon after school Tiffany came into the YMCA lounge and sat near Paul. Her blond hair was wet, so it had darkened to the color of caramel candy. Paul ignored her. He kept on ignoring her even when she jiggled up and down on the couch cushion and her wet hair showered him with water drops.

"I'm going to be in the Science Olympiad," said Tiffany. "That's like the Olympics, sort of, but for smart kids."

"So what? I'm going to be in it, too."

Tiffany bounced on the couch cushion, and her hair flounced so Paul could see her tiny gold earrings. "That's good. I'll see you there, then. Maybe we can eat lunch together like we did back when we went to the same school."

16

Eat lunch with Tiffany? Paul thought. Barf. That would be worse even than watching Billy eat.

"My school will probably win," Tiffany said. "I wonder what they'll give us. Maybe they'll give us a blue ribbon or a big gold trophy out of real gold. Or they could give us a trip to the Bahamas. That would be even better."

"It's just a contest between schools, stupid," Paul said in his most withering voice. "They aren't going to give us any trip to the Bahamas."

"I guess I'll find out when we win."

"Maybe you won't win."

"Why do you say that?" Tiffany turned her blue eyes on Paul. "Do you have some secret plan, Paul? If you do, you can tell me."

Paul cringed. He wished she wouldn't call him by his name like that, as if they were friends.

"Who else is going to be on your team?" Tiffany asked. "Is it anybody I know?"

"I'm not sure yet, but don't you worry," he said. "We're going to have a pretty good team."

"I'm going to be in the egg drop. What event are you going to be in?"

"The egg drop," he muttered.

"Neat!" exclaimed Tiffany.

Paul was beginning to regret his decision to be in the egg drop now that he knew Tiffany was planning to enter. But it was already set that Billy would build the mousetrap car. Paul could have switched to a completely different event, of course, like metric estimation or detect-a-substance. But none of the other events his father had mentioned sounded like as much fun as the mousetrap car and the egg drop.

"It'll be you against me," said Tiffany. "We'll get to see who has the best egg protector. It'll probably be me because I've already got some really great ideas."

"What kind of ideas?" asked Paul, curious in spite of himself.

"It's a secret!"

"You just don't have any ideas, that's all," said Paul.

A horn beeped at the front door, and Paul jumped up. His father's car was waiting outside.

"You'll see," sang Tiffany as Paul took off running. Paul's head felt warm. He was so angry he could hardly get the car door open. Boy, he wished he could make that Tiffany shut up just once.

The next morning Mrs. Hux announced the upcoming Science Olympiad. "I hope lots of you are going to sign up to work on this project, boys and girls," said Mrs. Hux. "Mrs. Melenik has volunteered to act as your adviser. The team will meet with her during our regular after-lunch story time."

Mrs. Hux thumbtacked a sheet of paper to the bulletin board. "Everyone who is interested in working on the Science Olympiad should sign up here," she said.

When the bell rang for recess, Paul went over to the bulletin board and signed up for the egg drop. He noticed that Carlos had signed up for the decathlon.

"What's a decathlon?" Paul asked him.

Carlos Perez shrugged. "Dunno. I guess I'll find out."

Paul looked at him in disgust. Happy-go-lucky types like Carlos were not the kind of players they needed. What they needed were kids who wanted to win.

When Paul went outside, he looked for Suzy. She was the type they needed. She hated to lose. Paul still remembered how she had "accidentally" dumped over the checkerboard last spring when she had been losing. He edged up to her. "You know what?" he said. "You ought to sign up for that science contest."

"Why?" asked Suzy. "Are you going to do it?"

"Sure. And, hey, you ought to do it, too."

Suzy fingered her braid, her eyes moving as she

watched the jump rope go around and around. Paul did not feel he had her full attention. He felt it was very important that he sign up smart kids like Suzy if their team was to be certain of beating Tiffany's new school. Paul suspected Tiffany was just bragging when she said her school always won everything, but he could not be sure of it. What if her school really did win everything? What if they were tough to beat?

"What do you say?" Paul asked. "You *ought* to do it, Suzy. We need you on the team."

"I don't know," Suzy said. "I'm not that crazy about science, actually."

"Look, they may call it a science contest, but it's really more like a game."

Suzy's gaze was still fixed on the twirling jump rope. Paul was afraid she wasn't really listening to him. Then he had an inspiration. "You and Kate ought to sign up together for that detect-a-substance event, you know, the one where you have to work as a pair? You two would be great together."

Suzy chewed on her lower lip. "Okay, maybe."

Paul smiled. He suddenly felt on a high, as if he had won the lottery. It had been smart of him to suggest Suzy and Kate could work as a team. They probably would have moved in together if their moms had let them.

"How does it work?" Suzy asked, looking at him.

Paul tried to recall all the things he knew about the Science Olympiad. His father had talked a good bit about it lately at the dinner table, but naturally Paul had paid attention mostly to the stuff about the egg-drop event and was a little hazy about the detect-a-substance event. "I think it's where they give you a bunch of things like salt and sugar and you have to tell what it is. It's like solving a mystery! It'll be real fun." Paul hoped his enthusiasm didn't sound forced. For a second there he had the awful sensation that he sounded like his mother when she was assuring him he would love going to visit Grandma Fenner.

Suzy ran toward the jump rope. "I'll ask Kate and see what she thinks!" she yelled over her shoulder.

Paul gave a little skip of excitement that kicked up a puff of dust at his feet. His team was getting a good start.

Paul's favorite piece of playground equipment was the oversize wooden pole that looked like a tree trunk. It had car tires nailed at intervals along its height to make it easy to climb. Paul scaled it quickly. Perched at the top, he looked down at the playground. He could feel the sun hot on his

hair and the trickle of sweat that was dripping down his back. From where Paul sat, the entire field was spread out below like a map. A few girls with Hula-Hoops were playing near the blackberry bushes that rimmed the field. On the patchy grass a bunch of kids were playing kickball. Over by the oak tree Paul could see Suzy jumping very fast—red-hot pepper. Near the chinning bars Carlos lay on a tire, looking up at the sky. Paul checked the sky himself, but there was no hang glider, no kite, no balloon. Nothing interesting at all was up there, only clouds. Carlos was actually spending recess looking at clouds! It was lucky for their team, Paul thought, that he was out stirring up interest. If they had to depend on guys like Carlos, they would be in pretty sad shape. Thinking of how he'd gotten Suzy to sign on, Paul began to feel a warm glow of certainty that his team was going to beat Tiffany's.

Chapter
Four

Paul studied the Science Olympiad rules carefully. The egg-drop directions alone filled a whole page. Large grade A eggs would be used, the instructions explained. Paul went into the kitchen and checked inside the refrigerator. No problem. He had almost a dozen large grade A eggs to practice on. Through the kitchen window he could see his mother and father cooking hamburgers on the grill while they talked across the fence to the neighbors. Smoke streamed up from the grill as Paul's father flipped over a burger.

Paul went back to his room and read the instructions some more. The package protecting the egg had to be less than 20 centimeters on a side, and it could weigh no more than 1 kilogram. Paul decided he would have to check with his father about that. They had studied metrics at school, but he had not paid much attention, so he was kind of unclear about exactly how much 20 centimeters and 1 kilogram were. The instructions also said that glass or metal could not be used. That made sense. Kids might get hurt if they started dropping glass or metal containers off the back of a bleacher. Finally Paul got to the last and most important paragraph, which told about the scoring.

Those eggs that survive without breakage or showing any detectable cracks will be scored. Ties will be broken by weight.

Paul gazed out his window, lost in thought. Lightness was obviously the important thing. What he needed was something to protect his egg that would be very light, as light as a feather.

Paul's own pillow was foam rubber because feathers made him sneeze, but his father had a feather pillow. He got a knife and a plastic bag from the kitchen, then went to his parents' room and carefully slit the end seam of his father's pillow. It was such a fat pillow he figured it had feathers to spare. When he pulled out a couple of handfuls of feathers and stuffed them in a plastic bag, a few floated out of the pillow and drifted down to the carpet. Paul picked up some of them, but they kept coming out. The pillow was leaking feathers at an alarming rate.

Quite a few feathers were floating around the room by now, blown by currents from the air-conditioning vents. Paul stapled the pillow closed with the stapler from his mother's desk. Then he picked up as many of the feathers as he could. There were an awful lot of them, but he figured since they were on the floor, they were not too noticeable.

Paul got an egg out of the refrigerator, put it in with the feathers, and tightened up the plastic bag with his fingers until he had a ball of feathers with an egg hidden inside. Then he put the bag on the kitchen counter and carefully stapled it shut. The perfect egg container. Now all he needed was a way to test it.

Too bad he did not live in a two-story house, he thought. It would have been so easy to drop it out a second-floor window.

Paul went in the living room and looked around for something tall that he could stand on. It was too bad that the ladder was out in the locked tool-shed. Paul didn't want to ask his dad to get it for him, because whenever his parents started helping him, the first thing they said was "Wait a minute, Paul." Then came the flurry of precautions. His parents spread out newspapers, fetched safety goggles, and insisted on reading directions until when Paul finally got around to doing whatever he had started to do, all the fun had gone out of it. Paul wanted to test his egg drop with no fuss. That meant he had to find the place to do it on his own.

Suddenly he noticed the piano. It was not as tall a dropping-off place as he would have liked, but it would have to do for now. He held tight to his egg package and stepped up on the piano stool. Before he knew it he was lying on his stomach on top of the upright piano. Unfortunately, his nose had begun to tickle, probably because of the feathers. Paul held his breath, inched closer to the edge of the piano, and counted to ten, trying not to think of his tickly nose. All at once he let go and his egg package fell. There was a sickening wet crunching sound as the egg package hit the floor. The plastic bag began to fill up with egg yolk and egg white. In a second the feathers inside looked wet and yucky. Paul was so depressed by this turn of events that he lay on his stomach staring at it, hardly noticing that the raw egg was leaking out between the staples. He sneezed loudly.

The back door swung shut. "Paul!" yelled his dad. "Dinnertime. Come and get it."

Paul knew his mother would not want him on top of the piano, so he began to scramble down. Unfortunately, the toe of his shoe caught on the cover of the piano keys, lifting it a bit, and his foot struck the keys with a dissonant crash.

"Paul!" exclaimed his mother. She was standing in the doorway staring up at him. "What on earth are you doing up on the piano?"

"Experimenting," he said. He slid down.

"You've been throwing eggs off the piano?" cried his mother, staring at the egg dribbling onto the carpet. "Onto my clean rug? This is not funny, Paul Alexander."

"Not throwing, dropping," Paul explained patiently. "How can I tell if my egg protector works unless I practice with real eggs?"

"What's the problem, you guys?" Mr. Fenner appeared at the door to the living room, spatula in hand. "Your hamburgers are getting cold."

Paul's mother glared.

"What did I do?" Mr. Fenner protested.

"Paul is practicing his egg drop for the Science Olympiad," Mrs. Fenner said.

Mr. Fenner looked down at the floor. A sticky yellow trickle was working its way under the piano. "Looks as if you've got a way to go, Paul."

"I guess feathers weren't such a great idea," Paul said.

"Are those feathers down there?" Mr. Fenner peered at the egg package. "Where on earth did you get feathers?"

Paul remembered the feathers fluttering around his parents' bedroom. He wondered if maybe the staples in the pillow had not been such a hot idea after all.

"I got them out of your pillow," he admitted.

"My down pillow?" cried Mr. Fenner.

Mr. Fenner ran into the bedroom to check on his pillow. His mother ran into the kitchen to get something to clean up the egg with. Paul didn't see why his parents had to make such a big deal about every little thing. He wondered what they would do in a real emergency if they got this steamed up over a single broken egg. He thought about pointing this out to them, but he sensed this was not the right moment.

Mrs. Fenner got to her knees and began wiping the raw egg off the carpet with a wet sponge. "Honestly, Paul!"

"I was just trying to do a scientific experiment," Paul said indignantly. "Boy, I'll bet if Einstein had had all this trouble he would never have gotten to be a famous scientist or anything."

A minute later Mr. Fenner came in clutching his pillow to his chest. "Emmy, do you think you can fix it?" he asked anxiously. "The pillow's been cut open, and for some reason or other it's full of staples." Mr. Fenner shot a reproachful look at Paul.

"Maybe we'd better just get you another one," Mrs. Fenner said wearily.

"I've had this pillow since I was in college," said Mr. Fenner mournfully. He buried his nose in it. "A new one just wouldn't be the same."

"I'll bet a new one would smell better," Paul said.

"Paul Alexander Fenner!" said his mother. "I don't want to hear another word out of you."

"It's nothing to me!" Paul said. "The dumb feathers don't work anyway."

Catching the look on his mother's face, Paul exited the room hastily. He went into the kitchen and began squirting ketchup on his hamburger.

After a while Paul's parents came into the kitchen and smiled brightly at him. Paul could tell they had been having a conference. He knew the signs. Whenever their faces wore matching expressions, it meant they had talked and decided to present a united front. He hated for them to gang up on him like that.

"I can see you need a place to practice your egg drops, Paul," said Mr. Fenner. "I'll put up the ladder in the carport for you."

"But you have to spread out newspapers," Mrs. Fenner added, "before you drop any eggs."

"We want you to enjoy the Science Olympiad, sport, but no more experimenting in the house. Is that understood?"

Paul nodded. "Can I spend the night over at

Billy's house? We need to work on his mousetrap car."

Mr. Fenner pulled out his chair and sat down at the kitchen table with a sigh. "It's wonderful to see you pitching in and getting to work on the contest like this, Paul. We admire your enthusiasm, don't we, Emmy?"

Paul's mother produced an unconvincing smile.

Chapter
Five

"Ouch!" Paul carefully lifted the bar of the mousetrap and released his finger. "Wow, I've heard about mousetraps, but I didn't realize that was how they worked."

"They've got to have a hair trigger," explained Billy, "or else they wouldn't go off when a mouse nibbles on the cheese." Billy pulled the wire bar back and reset the trap.

"You don't have to reset it," said Paul. "I see how it works."

"Ouch!" cried Billy as the trap snapped. He detached his finger from the trap and shook it. "Boy, these things go off at the least little thing."

"Don't set it!" Paul warned. "We can't work on it if it's always snapping at us."

Paul pulled the rear wheels off a small toy car and examined them. "Our big problem is going to be to glue the wheels on the mousetrap so that they can turn. If we just glue the axle to the mousetrap, see, then the wheels won't turn. They'll be stuck in one place by the glue."

"Dad-dy!" yelled Billy.

"Why did you have to do that?" asked Paul. "We can figure it out on our own." He knew what would happen now. Mr. Blakely would come in and tell them to "wait a minute." Paul had decided that "Wait a minute" was his least favorite phrase in the English language. It ranked right up there with "The assignment for this weekend is . . ."

Mr. Blakely strode into the kitchen. He didn't dress like any of the other fathers Paul knew. Maybe it was because he worked in the advertising business, but he did not wear scruffy old clothes like Paul's father or suits with matching vests like Suzy's father. Instead he wore T-shirts that buttoned up the front and baggy, acid-washed jeans. "Hi, kids," he said. "How's it going?"

"We need to glue the wheels on the mousetrap so that they'll still turn, and we can't figure out how," said Billy.

"We just got started, for pete's sake," muttered Paul. "We can figure it out."

Mr. Blakely put on his glasses and looked closely at the pair of wheels Paul had snapped off the toy car. "There's an easier way to do this, kids. I think I've got some wheels in an old erector set up in the attic. They're made to order for something like this."

"Aw-right!" Billy said excitedly. "Let's get 'em."

"Wait a minute." Mr. Blakely held up his hand.

There it is, thought Paul. The inevitable "Wait a minute" that made his palms and feet itch with impatience.

"I'm not going to troop up into the attic at this time of night, gang. It's time for you to turn in. I'll go up and look for them tomorrow morning. You'll still have plenty of time to work on the car."

"Oh, Daddy!"

"Don't start, Billy. It's ten-thirty. Now, why don't you two go brush your teeth and get ready for bed?"

"I knew we shouldn't have watched *A Nightmare on Elm Street,*" said Paul. "We would have had plenty of time if we had started to work on the mousetraps right away when I first came over."

"You were the one who wanted to watch it," said Billy.

Paul had to admit that was true. His parents would never have let him watch anything so unsuitable, so if he wanted to see it, he had to grab his chance while he could. But it was too bad that they couldn't work some more on the mousetrap tonight. It wouldn't have killed Mr. Blakely to go up in the attic.

"What's the big deal?" said Billy. "We'll get the wheels tomorrow."

When Paul got started on something, he liked to go ahead and *do* it. Half the people in the world, it seemed like all they wanted to do was *talk* about doing something. Paul sighed.

"We'll get started on it first thing in the morning," promised Billy.

Chapter
Six

Mr. Blakely brought the erector set wheels down from the attic right after breakfast. Paul saw immediately that they were perfect for the mousetrap car. They had been constructed to be easily attached to things. An extra bit of plastic was already wrapped around the axle for that purpose. When the extra plastic was glued to the mousetrap, the wheels would still be able to move freely.

"Here we go, boys." Mr. Blakely shook his hair out of his eyes with a backward toss of his head. "All we have to do now is glue them on the mousetrap and we're in business," he said. "Get the glue for me, will you, Billy?"

Paul followed him into the kitchen while Billy went off to find the glue. Paul wished Billy's father would get out of the way. Why couldn't he hand the wheels over to Billy and go back to reading the morning paper?

"Here you go, Dad." Billy laid a tube of glue on the kitchen table.

Mr. Blakely put a few drops of glue onto the bottom of the mousetrap and attached the wheels. Paul watched him closely. "We can glue on the other set of wheels ourselves," he said as soon as Mr. Blakely had finished.

"Better not," said Mr. Blakely. "This epoxy glue is kind of tricky." He glued the second set of wheels to the back of the mousetrap and set it down on the table. Now the mousetrap looked like a toy car. True, it was a funny-looking sort of car since it had nothing but a mousetrap for a chassis. But when nudged, it rolled along the kitchen table the way any other toy car would have.

"Great!" exclaimed Billy. "Now all we need is to tie a string to the bar so that when the spring snaps it shut, mousetrap power will make it go."

"Piece of cake." Mr. Blakely smiled. "But first we'd better wrap the axle with masking tape. See, boys, when we tie the string to the axle, it's going to slip and not make those wheels turn unless we give it something to hold on to. The masking tape will give us some traction." Mr. Blakely pulled open a kitchen drawer and got out a fat roll of masking tape.

Paul couldn't believe the way Mr. Blakely was taking over their project. He stared at the ceiling while Mr. Blakely wrapped masking tape around the shiny metal axle. He was afraid if he looked right at him, he would stick out his tongue. What drove Paul crazy was that Mr. Blakely hadn't let them do a single thing. And worse yet, Billy didn't even seem to mind.

When Mr. Blakely had finished wrapping the tape, Paul said, "We can do the rest. Can't we, Billy?"

Mr. Blakely didn't pay any attention to him. "Do you know where the string is, Billy?" he asked.

"Sure!" said Billy. He ran out of the kitchen and appeared a moment later with a ball of string.

"Thanks, son," said Mr. Blakely. He tied the string around the bar connected to the spring. "Now we need to measure the string. Get me a ruler." Mr. Blakely was bent over the mousetrap, his hair falling forward so that Paul could barely make out what he was doing.

"Here's the ruler," Billy said, running breathlessly into the kitchen with it.

"Great," said Mr. Blakely. "Careful measurements, that's the important thing."

"I can measure it," put in Paul. "I know how."

"I know you can, Paul, but this has to be absolutely exact." Mr. Blakely pulled the string out against the ruler. "Scissors?" he asked. He held out his hand.

Billy got a pair of scissors and put them in his father's hand. "It's really coming along, isn't it?" Billy said proudly.

Paul didn't say anything. He personally thought that Mr. Blakely was a buttinsky. Of course, he couldn't say that. He was a guest at Billy's house, so he had to be polite. But he could feel the word *butt-insky* poised on the tip of his tongue.

Mr. Blakely pushed the spring bar of the mousetrap back into the "set" position. Peering at it closely, he tied the other end of the string around the axle. Snap! Suddenly the mousetrap snapped shut.

Paul whooped. He had to cover his mouth to make himself stop laughing. The mousetrap car was dangling from Mr. Blakely's hair. Mr. Blakely clumsily pried the mousetrap car free, saying several of the words that the Family Channel always blipped.

"Are you okay, Dad?" asked Billy.

Mr. Blakely threw the mousetrap car onto the kitchen table and ran his fingers through his hair. "I guess some of my hair got caught in the spring," he said grimly. "That's why I had a little trouble getting it off. Anyway, now we're done. The car's finished."

39

"Aw-right!" exclaimed Billy.

"Why don't you boys test it?" suggested Mr. Blakely.

Paul knew that the only reason they were getting to test it was because Mr. Blakely did not want to get close to the mousetrap again. It was too bad the trap hadn't snapped at him earlier, before he finished the entire project.

Billy put the mousetrap car down on the kitchen's vinyl floor and set it. Then he touched the trap gently with a spoon. The trap snapped shut, the string pulled on the axle, making the wheels turn, and the car sped across the kitchen floor.

"Look at that!" cried Billy. "We did it! It really went a long way, didn't it, Paul?"

"Pretty far," admitted Paul.

"It needs a little graphite on the wheels," Mr. Blakely said. "That'll cut down on the friction. We can probably get more distance that way."

"I bet we're going to win!" cried Billy. "Hey, you were right, Paul. This is fun! It was easy."

Paul couldn't believe that Billy thought he had done the mousetrap car all by himself. All he had done was to hand things to his father. Paul would not have dreamed of letting his father help him like that with his egg protector. If he won a prize, it was going to mean something.

He got lost for a moment in the vision of him-

41

self walking up to the platform to receive his blue ribbon, but he brought himself up short. He had hardly even begun his project. That disaster with the feathers meant, unfortunately, back to the old drawing board. And he didn't have a clue how to begin. He wondered if Tiffany really did have a lot of good ideas the way she said. He could have used even one good idea. "I think I'd better go home now," he said uneasily.

"You're going home already?" asked Billy in surprise.

"I've got a lot of work to do."

"I thought you were going to stay until after lunch."

"I have to work on my project. I'm just getting started."

"You ought to bring it over here. My dad could help you with it the way he helped me with mine."

The idea of Mr. Blakely helping him with his project made the skin on the back of Paul's neck prickle, but he forced himself to speak calmly. "That's okay," he said. "I can do it. It's just that I'd really better be getting home."

Mrs. Blakely gave Paul a ride back to his house.

"Back so soon, sweetheart?" Mrs. Fenner called to him from the kitchen. "I thought you were going to stay at Billy's for lunch."

Paul found his mother cutting up an orange over the kitchen sink. "Do you want some breakfast?" she asked.

"I ate at Billy's." Paul made a face.

"You look pretty grumpy, sweetheart. What happened? Didn't you have a good time?"

"Billy's dumb dad did the entire mousetrap car for us," Paul burst out, "and Billy acted like he had done it himself! It's like he can't even tell the difference, Mom."

"Lots of parents help kids with their projects, Paul. It's not such a big deal. Just because it's not the way we do things around here doesn't mean it's actually wrong."

"I'm not talking *help*. I'm talking about him doing every single thing."

"It sounds as if Art Blakely got kind of carried away."

"I'll say!"

Paul went to his room and lay on his bed for a while, staring at the ceiling and thinking of how fragile eggs were. It was something he had been thinking about a lot lately. At the store eggs came in special foam plastic containers that were supposed to keep them from breaking. Each egg rested in its own plastic foam cup, but Paul didn't think that method worked too well. He had noticed that his mother always opened an egg carton

43

and checked each egg to make sure none had been broken before she bought it. Also, Paul had seen foam egg cartons laid aside at the store with dribbles of dried yellow yolk on the containers, so obviously some had broken. And that was without their getting dropped off a bleacher like the eggs in the contest. He knew he needed something better than the foam plastic containers eggs came in. Maybe a thicker sort of foam would do. But where could he get such a thing?

Chapter
Seven

Paul hoped an idea for an egg protector would come to him all of a sudden when he wasn't thinking about it. He went into his parents' room and dialed Suzy's number. Not that he was crazy about the idea of calling up a girl. If you did it more than once or twice, people were apt to go around saying that you liked her. But he wasn't getting anywhere with his own project, and working on Billy's mousetrap car had turned out to be a big zero. He figured it would cheer him up to hear that Suzy and Kate were making progress with their project.

"May I speak to Suzy, please?" asked Paul when Mr. Hart picked up the phone. "This is Paul." Mr. Hart yelled "Su-zy, it's Paul," at the top of his voice. Paul wished he hadn't told him his name. This was embarrassing.

"Hello?" said Suzy.

"I'm just calling to check up on how you and Kate are doing with your project for the science contest," Paul said.

"It's coming along just great," said Suzy. "Mrs. Hux gave us a list of all the things we have to identify, and Kate and I have been practicing. We can identify salt and sugar every time perfectly. But we're still having trouble telling baking powder from plaster of Paris. Cornstarch and flour are tricky, too. It would be easy if you could taste the stuff, but you aren't allowed. How's your project coming?"

"I've got some ideas," said Paul. "But I still haven't worked out the details."

"Billy just called me. He's got his mousetrap car completely finished. He said he put graphite on the wheels, and now it goes a real long way."

Paul was startled. Billy had called Suzy? He wondered if that meant Billy liked Suzy. Nah! That couldn't be.

"I'm just glad graphite isn't one of the things we have to identify," Suzy said. "I don't even know what it is."

Paul didn't, either, but he didn't see any reason to go into that now. "Billy's father helped him a lot with his mousetrap," he said. He felt disloyal as soon as he said it, but it was true.

"Maybe so," said Suzy, "but at least he's fin-

46

ished with his. I wish Kate and I were finished. Are you going to Skate World tonight?"

The question took Paul by surprise. He had so much on his mind, he had completely forgotten about his school's fund-raising project at Skate World. A couple of times a year the roller-skating rink held a school night, and participating schools got half the ticket price for each of their students who attended. Paul had gone last year and had had a good time. "Sure, I'm going. I forgot to tell my mom about it, but she'll take me. I'll be there."

"Great," said Suzy. "Maybe we can skate together when they do couples only."

Talk about *embarrassing*. Paul hoped Suzy wasn't getting the wrong idea about this call. "Well, I just wanted to know how your project was coming along," he said hastily. "See ya."

Paul heard his mother in the hall. "Mom!" he yelled. "I've got to go to this thing at Skate World tonight."

"I didn't know you had something you had to do tonight." His mother peeked her head in the kitchen door. "I wish you would remember to put these things on the family calendar, Paul."

"You can drive me, can't you?"

"Sure. No problem. Would you check the mail, Paul?"

Paul liked going out by the street to get the mail

out of the box. Sometimes interesting things had arrived, like postcards from foreign countries. His grandmother traveled a good bit, and he had gotten a lot of good stamps off her postcards. Today a brown package was in the mailbox. Paul shook it gently, but it didn't rattle. It didn't even rustle. Also, it was addressed to his dad. Too bad. Paul leafed through the bills and circulars. It was not a good day for mail. Today there weren't even any free soap samples.

When Paul took the mail into the house, his father noticed the brown package. "That must be my tapes," said Mr. Fenner. "Toss it here, Paul. I got a new recording of the Brandenburg Concertos." Mr. Fenner tore open the package.

Paul watched as his father took two small cassettes out of the box. They were swathed round and round with plastic bubble wrap and secured with tape.

"Dad, can I have that?" asked Paul.

Mr. Fenner looked surprised. "I didn't know you were interested in classical music, Paul."

"No, I mean the box and all the packing stuff."

Mrs. Fenner laughed. "Isn't that always the way of it? The box is more interesting than what comes in it. I remember when I was your age, Paul, I had the most wonderful time playing with an old refrigerator box."

Paul stuffed the bubble wrap and wadded-up bits of paper back in the cardboard box. "Mom, you won't forget I've got to go to Skate World at six, will you?"

"We've got a lot of time until then, Paul."

"I know. I'm just reminding you."

As soon as Paul got to his room, he sat down on his bed to gloat over his bubble wrap. He was sure it was perfect for the egg protector. He lifted the cardboard box with one hand. It was too big to use, he decided. Even if it were a bit smaller, it would still have been too heavy. He remembered those important words in the instructions—"Ties will be broken by weight." It was extremely important that his egg protector be light. That was the great thing about the bubble wrap. Nothing was lighter than bubble wrap except for air. After all, mostly bubble wrap *was* air, air trapped between thin sheets of plastic wrap. It was perfect, absolutely perfect. All he needed was some kind of container for it.

Paul dived into his closet. He kept all kinds of things there because he never knew what might turn out to be useful. A moment later he considered the pile of odds and ends he had heaped on his bedroom floor—an empty tennis ball can, an old sock, a crayon box, a box of modeling clay. All were containers of one sort or another, yet

49

none seemed quite right for the egg. Then he spotted a cone-shaped party hat in the corner of his closet. It was light and somewhat larger than an egg but not too large. It was just big enough, Paul judged, to hold a large grade A egg that had been wrapped around several times with bubble wrap.

He ran into the kitchen.

"Paul," Mrs. Fenner called. "What are you up to?"

"Nothing!"

"Paul," Mr. Fenner warned, "remember, we talked about that. No more practicing with the eggs except on the carport with plenty of newspaper."

"And this is *not* a good time for you to practice," added Mrs. Fenner.

"I'm not doing anything," protested Paul. "I'm just thinking."

Paul quietly removed an egg from the refrigerator and stashed it under his shirt. It felt so cold he almost giggled. The precaution of sticking it under his shirt was necessary just in case his mother decided to check on him. Going slowly, he moved out of the kitchen while holding on to the egg through his shirt. At last he closed his bedroom door behind him and sighed with relief. He sat down on the floor and wrapped the egg up in the bubble wrap. He used all the layers of bubble wrap he had, then stuffed the entire bundle into the cone-shaped party hat. To his relief it just fit. The only problem was that he needed to have some way to make sure it all stayed put. But that problem was easily solved. With the egg snug and safe inside the bubble wrap, he would staple the wrap to the hat. He would just have to be very careful not to break the egg when he did his stapling. Paul carefully unwrapped the egg and tiptoed back to the kitchen and opened the refrigerator.

"Paul?" Paul was convinced his mother could hear the refrigerator door open at fifty yards. She had ears like a bat. "If you're hungry," she called, "there are cinnamon rolls on top of the refrigerator."

"I'm just getting a glass of orange juice!" Paul yelled.

Happiness swelled inside him like a balloon as he went back to his room. At last he had a good idea. And not just a good idea, an absolutely terrific, wonderful, great idea!

After supper Mrs. Fenner drove Paul to Skate World. Kids stood in a clump at the ticket window waiting their turn.

"Hey, Paul!" Tiffany waved at him as he got out of the car.

Oh, no! Paul hadn't thought about how other schools would be at Skate World tonight and that there was a chance of running into Tiffany. He had the impulse to jump back in the car, but Billy and Suzy had already spotted him. Anyway, he reminded himself, why should he mind running into Tiffany? He had a great idea for his egg protector. It was probably a whole lot better than any of hers.

Paul put his hands in his pockets and strolled over to the other kids. "Hi," he said.

"How's your project coming?" asked Tiffany.

"I've already finished mine," said Billy. *"Varoom!"* He made a sweeping motion with his hand. "It's a mousetrap car, and it really goes a long way."

"Paul and I are doing the egg protector," said Tiffany.

Paul rolled his eyes. Tiffany made it sound as if they were working together. "I've almost finished mine," he said. He pushed his money toward the ticket vendor. "This afternoon I got a really great idea."

Kids streamed inside the door. Rock music was blaring over a loudspeaker. Strobe lights flashing over the dim skating rink made Paul feel dizzy. He and Billy went over to get their roller skates. It took Paul some time to get his skates laced up, so he had no choice but to listen to Tiffany when she sat down beside him and began talking.

"What's your egg protector like, Paul?" asked Tiffany. "What are you using to make yours?"

"It's a secret," said Paul.

"Yeah," said Billy. "If he told you, you might steal his idea."

"I don't need to steal his idea, dummy," said Tiffany. "I have plenty of ideas of my own. You should be glad somebody's interested in your stupid egg protector, Paul."

"Don't do me any favors, huh, Tiffany?" said Paul.

Suzy sat on the carpeted bench and began lacing up her skates. "Hi, Tiffany. How do you like your new school?"

"I love it," said Tiffany loudly. "It's the best school in the city."

"That's nice," said Suzy. "Has anybody seen Kate? She ought to be here already." Paul couldn't believe that Suzy didn't seem to mind Tiffany's bragging about her new school. She was hardly even paying attention.

Jeff Taggert skated clumsily over to the bench where Paul sat. His face was pink, his hair was damp near his temples, and he looked as if he needed to rest. Suzy giggled when he sat down.

"What's with you?" Jeff asked. His hair was slicked back in a new way. Paul knew he was worried that Suzy was laughing at his hair.

"I was just thinking," Suzy said, "that somebody around here will be glad to see you."

"Who?" asked Tiffany.

"Kate," whispered Suzy in her ear. "She likes Jeff."

"What?" asked Jeff nervously. He was still worried that they were talking about his hair.

"I was just saying that Kate likes you," said Suzy.

"Are you and Kate going together?" Tiffany asked Jeff.

"No!" said Jeff, alarmed. He got up abruptly and skated off.

Paul had just about finished lacing up his skates when he saw Kate. Just about every part of Skate World was carpeted except the rink itself, so once a person stepped out of the rink it was pretty slow going. It took Kate a couple of minutes to work her way over to them. "I wish you could have come earlier," she told Suzy. "I've already been here for ages."

"My mom said I had to eat supper first. You just missed Jeff. He was sitting right next to me."

"Where is he?" asked Kate, looking around.

"He's in the bathroom," said Paul, who thought things were getting interesting.

"I'm going to go get a snow cone," said Kate. She nudged Suzy. "Why don't you come with me to get a snow cone, huh?"

"I just got here," protested Suzy. "I don't want a snow cone yet."

Kate stamped her skate. "Suzy!"

Suzy pushed herself up off the bench with a sigh. "Okay, let's go get a snow cone." The refreshment pavilion was right next to the bathrooms. It was pretty obvious to Paul that Kate planned to keep an eye out for Jeff. That was why she wanted to get a snow cone.

"Let's skate," said Paul.

He and Billy got up and made their way to the rink. Tiffany followed right behind them. "I can't get away from that girl no matter what I do," complained Paul.

"What girl?" asked Billy. The music had a strong beat and was very loud.

"Tiffany," said Paul.

When they stepped out onto the rink, Tiffany wheeled around in a circle and began skating backward.

"Look at that!" said Billy, impressed. "Can you skate backward like that, Paul?"

"I could, I guess, if I wanted to, but I don't want to," said Paul.

A boy bumped into Tiffany, and they both fell down. Skaters had to quickly step aside to avoid hitting them.

Paul immediately felt better. That would teach her to show off. "Let's go," he said.

Paul loved skating. He was not sure he could

skate backward like Tiffany. The truth was that
he found stopping without crashing hard enough.
But he liked the crowds of kids wheeling past him,
the noise, the darkness, the music. He liked everything about Skate World except that their snow
cones cost too much.

After they had been skating a while, Billy called,
"Jeff is still in the bathroom."

"What did you say?" asked Paul. He skated
closer to Billy so he could hear him better.

"I said Jeff is still in the bathroom," Billy
repeated.

"How can you be sure? Maybe he left and you
didn't see him."

"I've been watching," said Billy. "Look over
there. Suzy and Kate are still eating snow cones."

Paul had to admit that probably meant Jeff was
still in the bathroom because if he had come out,
Kate would have chased after him.

"Maybe we'd better check on him," said Paul.
"What if he's sick?"

The boys skated around the rink until they got
to the bathroom. This time when Paul tried to
stop, he bumped against the side of the rink so
hard that his teeth clicked together. At least, he
thought with relief, he didn't run into anybody.

Paul and Billy skated around the tall wooden
screen that shielded the door to the bathroom.

Torn paper towels with skate marks on them were stuck to the tile floor of the bathroom. Jeff stood in the corner, his face a blank.

"What are you doing, man?" asked Paul. "You've been in here forever."

"I'm waiting for Suzy and Kate to leave," said Jeff. "Are they still out there?"

Billy skated outside the bathroom, then returned promptly with his report. "They're still there."

"Look, you can't stay in the bathroom all night," said Paul.

"Sure, I can."

"Look," said Paul after a moment's thought, "what if I block Kate when she starts after you so you can get away?"

Jeff brightened. "Okay." He was obviously pretty tired of standing there in the corner of the bathroom, thought Paul. Who wouldn't be?

"Well, here goes," said Jeff.

As soon as Jeff skated out of the bathroom, Kate and Suzy leapt up from their seats and headed after him. Paul made a beeline in their direction. It was difficult to skate recklessly on the carpeted floor, but he did manage to succeed in bumping into Kate.

"Oomph," said Kate. She grabbed at the arch-way of the refreshment pavilion to keep her balance. "Watch where you're going, Paul!" Kate looked up in time to see Jeff skate out onto the rink. "Oh, my gosh, he's gotten away, Suzy. It's like he's trying to escape from me!"

"Of course he's trying to get away from you," said Paul. "Suzy told him that you liked him. What'd you expect?"

"You did that, Suzy?" cried Kate. Tears sprang to her eyes. "How *could* you?"

"Well, you *do* like him," Suzy said helplessly. "How could I know he was going to run away from you?"

"Couples only!" boomed the voice over the loudspeaker. "Couples only for this song. Clear the floor, please. Couples only."

Paul saw Jeff cast a frightened look over his shoulder. Suddenly Jeff grabbed Tiffany's hand. Paul watched in astonishment as Jeff and Tiffany skated away to some dreamy music. Paul was sure Jeff had grabbed Tiffany's hand only as a way of making sure Kate wouldn't ask him to skate with her.

Kate wiped her eyes with her sleeve. "I hate you, Suzy Hart. It's all your fault."

"It is not!" cried Suzy.

"Don't you ever speak to me again!" said Kate. In short, angry steps she skated away on the carpet.

Suzy wheeled around to face Paul. "Why did

you have to go tell her that I told Jeff she liked him?"

Paul shrugged. "How was I supposed to know it was some big secret?" He looked over at Kate. She was standing at the pay telephone by snow cone counter. She was probably calling her mother to come pick her up.

"Ooo," Suzy said. "Paul Fenner, you are just awful."

At least, thought Paul with satisfaction, now he didn't have to worry about Suzy asking him to skate the couples-only set with her.

Chapter
Eight

Monday, at school, the rumor went around that Kate was threatening to squirt Suzy all over with perfume so she would stink so much no one would come near her. Paul was inclined to believe this threat because he had seen Kate before school taking a few practice squirts with an atomizer.

"I think Kate's still mad at you," he told Suzy when he saw her by the water fountain.

Suzy didn't say anything, but she looked upset.

"You two had better make up pretty soon," he said, "because you need to practice together for the contest."

"All you think about is that stupid contest," said Suzy. "There are a lot of other things that are more important, you know."

Offhand, Paul couldn't think of any. More than anything he wanted to be able to laugh in Tiffany's face the next time she said that her school was the best. "Oh, yeah?" he would say when she started to brag. "If you're so hot, how come you didn't win the Science Olympiad, huh?" That would shut her up.

At recess Paul saw Kate jumping rope. He noticed that Suzy had gone over to play kickball. He happened to know that Suzy hated playing kickball, so this meant the argument between the girls was serious.

Kate jumped ten times, then missed. When she ran out of the rope, she nearly ran right into Paul.

"Hey, watch where you're going," he said.

"You don't have to stand right by the jump rope," Kate answered.

"Come on, Kate, when are you and Suzy going to make up?"

"Never!" Kate's face darkened. "I am never going to speak to Suzy Hart again in my whole life, and you can tell her I said so!"

"But you two need to practice for the science contest."

"Oh, go away, Paul."

Paul couldn't believe that after all his careful efforts to build up a good team, it was falling apart before his very eyes. How were Suzy and Kate going to polish up their detect-a-substance performance and learn to tell cornstarch from flour if they weren't even speaking to each other? Paul was afraid they weren't practicing at all. All they were thinking about was this stupid fight.

Paul was still brooding on the problem after recess, when Mrs. Hux went around the room asking people what kind of audiovisual presentation they were going to do for their state project. Paul's state was Vermont. He wondered if Mrs. Hux would let him use a can of maple syrup as his audiovisual aid. He decided not to mention that idea just yet, but to see what she said about other people's ideas first. He wanted to see if anybody got shot down.

"Suzy, what do you plan to do?" asked Mrs. Hux.

"My state is Arizona and I plan to do a model of the Grand Canyon."

A bunch of girls in the back of the room giggled. Paul turned around and looked at them. He couldn't see what was so funny about a model of the Grand Canyon. Suzy's ears turned red, but she went on with determination. "I'm going to make it out of papier-mâché and show all the different strata and what grows at each level."

This made Paul's maple syrup idea look pretty silly, he thought. He decided that when Mrs. Hux asked him, he would say he hadn't come up with an idea yet. After all, he had been pretty busy working on his egg protector. He hadn't been able to spend much time thinking about audiovisuals. He noticed that the girls in the back of the room were laughing harder than ever.

"Is there something funny that you girls would like to share with the rest of us?" asked Mrs. Hux severely.

Kate and the other girls shook their heads, but they grinned broadly. Suzy did not look around. It hit Paul then that Kate had organized the girls at the back of the class to laugh at Suzy. It seemed to be a pretty good revenge. Suzy looked as if she was about to cry.

It was Friday, the day Paul's dad left work early, so Paul did not go to the Y for swimming after school. He waited to catch a ride home with the car pool, but Mrs. Hart was late. Paul and Billy stood at the curb discussing possible audiovisual projects. "Maybe if along with the maple syrup I took in some maple candy, it would be okay," Paul said. Just then he saw Suzy. "Hey, where've you been? You and Kate making up, maybe?" he asked hopefully.

Suzy's eyes narrowed to slits. "Kate is my enemy. You saw what she did to me today. She's turning everybody against me."

"Oh, come on," said Paul, "it's no big deal."

"Not *everybody's* against you, Suzy," Billy put in.

"Practically everybody," snapped Suzy. "You don't know what it's like to have an enemy, Billy. You're lucky."

"I thought you two were such big friends," Paul protested. Mrs. Hart's station wagon pulled up to the curb, and Suzy pulled the door of the car open. "That was before she turned against me," she said. "I know what I'm going to do. I'm going to have a big slumber party, and I'm going to ask everybody, all my friends, except for her."

Mrs. Hart tossed a magazine under the seat to make room for Suzy to sit beside her. "Did you have a nice day?" she asked.

To Paul's horror, as soon as Suzy closed the car door, she burst into tears.

"You didn't have a nice day?" asked Mrs. Hart, bewildered.

"Don't worry, Suzy," Paul reassured her. "We were already driving away. Nobody saw you cry."

"Don't speak to me, Paul Fenner!" cried Suzy.

"Suzy!" exclaimed Mrs. Hart. "What's the matter with you?"

"I don't want to talk about it," Suzy said in a low voice.

They rode the rest of the drive home in silence. Paul was forced to admit to himself that the chances of Suzy and Kate making up soon did not look good. And the Science Olympiad was this very Saturday!

As soon as Paul got home, he got an egg and wrapped it up in his egg protector. Then he got his dad to unlock the storage room and help him set up the ladder on the carport. If Suzy and Kate were flaking out on him, it was more important than ever that his egg protector be a winning entry. His team needed all the points it could get.

"What's the decathlon exactly, Dad?" Paul asked.

"Well, in the Olympics the decathlon is a contest made up of ten different events and the guy with the highest score overall wins the gold.

"But at the Science Olympiad it's a kind of race where the kids answer questions. The contestant goes to the first station, answers a question there, then hurries to the next station to answer a question there, and so forth. The contestants are graded on the time it takes them and on the number of questions they answer correctly."

Paul tried to imagine Carlos hurrying, but he couldn't. "My egg protector better win," he muttered. "We're going to need the points."

"Why don't I steady the ladder for you?" suggested his dad.

"Okay," said Paul. He climbed up it holding his egg package with its egg swaddled in bubble wrap and neatly stapled in place inside the party

hat. When he reached the next to the top step of the ladder, he leaned over and dropped his package onto the newspaper-covered concrete below. It fell lightly onto the paper and then rolled in a semicircle. Paul scrambled down the ladder.

"Wait a minute, now," said Mr. Fenner. "What's your hurry?"

Paul snatched up the party hat and looked at it. The egg was barely visible under so many layers of bubble wrap, but it was still whole.

"It didn't break!" he crowed. "I've done it!"

"Good work!" said his father.

And, thought Paul with satisfaction, I did it all by myself.

Monday at school Kate and Suzy were still fighting. In the afternoon Kate missed her social studies book. "I had it this morning!" she cried.

"Are you sure you didn't leave it at home?" asked Mrs. Hux.

"I had it before lunch when we did social studies," said Kate.

Mrs. Hux gave the class a stern look. "Boys and girls, has anybody seen Kate's social studies book?"

All the children shook their heads.

"Well," said Mrs. Hux, "it has to be in this room somewhere, and nobody is going home until we find it."

The bell rang, but nobody dared to move with Mrs. Hux giving the whole class such an awful look.

"Wait a minute, Mrs. Hux," said Suzy. "I think I see it! Over in the book nook. It's right behind that cushion."

Paul didn't see anything, but Suzy went over to the book nook and got a social studies book from behind one of the cushions. "I could just see a corner of it peeking out," she explained. She handed it to Kate with a smile.

Kate looked at her coldly. "Thank you."

"All right, boys and girls," said Mrs. Hux, "you may go now."

As they left the classroom, Paul groaned. "Suzy and Kate are so busy being enemies they've forgotten all about the contest, and Carlos is a million miles away in some dream world. Our team is a mess."

"My mousetrap car is all ready to go, though," said Billy proudly.

"Yeah," said Paul with little enthusiasm. He hated to be reminded of the mousetrap car.

Thursday afternoon Paul saw Kate approaching his house on her bicycle. "I guess she's going over to Suzy's," he said to himself. "Maybe she's going to plant a bomb or something."

Paul ran out to the road and flagged Kate down. She put her foot on the sidewalk and slowed the bicycle to a stop.

"Well, what is it, Paul?"

"Nothing," he said. "I just thought that if you happened to be going over in the direction of Suzy's house, you might want to stop in there and practice for the contest some."

"I'm just going over there to get my pencils, the ones with my name on them. I left them over there." Kate shifted her weight and blinked uneasily.

"You figure it's okay?" Paul tilted his head. "I mean, I thought you guys were sort of not getting along."

"I called Suzy up," Kate said, "and she said I could come on over." But she looked uncertain.

Paul thought hard. Could Suzy be setting some kind of booby trap for Kate? Why else would she lure her enemy over to her house. Nah, he decided. Suzy was too nice to do anything like that. Besides, she probably didn't have any idea how to make a booby trap. If it had been him, he could have thought of six or eight good booby traps. Everything from the jungle tiger trap (except you needed a big hole and some pointed stakes for that) to the old reliable bag of flour on top of the door. But he couldn't see Suzy pulling any of those stunts. "It's good you're going over there," he said. "Yeah, real good. Because if you happen to get a chance, you could put in a little practice for the contest. It's coming up this Saturday, you know. We don't have much time."

"All you think about is that contest," said Kate. Lowering her eyebrows at him, she suddenly hopped on her bike and sped away.

Paul would have loved to know what was happening over at Suzy's. When he went inside, he leaned on the windowsill and peered wistfully out the window, aching to do something. He wished at least that he had X-ray vision and could see through the pine trees and the other houses and right into Suzy's house.

Finally, unable to sit still, he went into the kitchen and dialed Suzy's number. Suzy answered the phone. "Hullo?"

"Suzy, this is Paul. I just wanted to remind you that the contest is this Saturday. That's the day after tomorrow."

"I know."

"Well, I just wanted to remind you. 'Bye." Paul hung up. Suzy hadn't sounded angry. She hadn't sounded exactly happy, either. He sighed. He couldn't figure out exactly what she *had* sounded like.

Chapter
Nine

Saturday morning Paul's mother had to work, so his father took him to the parking lot of the school. Most of the team had already arrived. Paul was surprised to see that Suzy and Kate were standing by Mrs. Melenik's van giggling together.

Billy scratched his head. "I guess they aren't enemies anymore."

"They must have made up. I wonder if they've been practicing," said Paul. "I mean, I wonder if they ever got so they could tell the cornstarch and the whatchamacallit apart."

"Dunno," said Billy.

Paul's father patted him on the back. "Good luck, kids."

"We'll need it," said Paul, glancing meaningfully at Carlos.

"I'll see you there," added Paul's father. "I'm going to help with some of the events."

A few minutes later the kids all got in the van and rode to the local college, where the competition was to be held.

"People," Mrs. Melenik said when they arrived, "consult your maps to learn how to find each event. If you get lost, the students wearing red T-shirts can give you directions." She smiled gaily. "See you at the awards ceremony! That's in the auditorium. Check your schedules."

Paul glanced at his photocopied schedule. When he saw "awards ceremony" listed, butterflies fluttered in his stomach. He hoped his team would be getting some awards. He hated to think of having to face Tiffany without a single blue ribbon.

"The egg drop isn't until ten o'clock," Billy pointed out. "You can come with me while I do mine, okay?"

The boys walked together to the gymnasium where the mousetrap car competition was to be held. Since Paul's father taught at the college Paul had been on campus lots of times and knew his way around. He did not even have to look at the map he had been given.

When they went into the gymnasium, at first it seemed half of the fourth graders in the city were lined up at one end of it.

"Boy, there are a lot of people in this one." Billy licked his lips.

"Don't worry," Paul said, glancing around. "A lot of these guys are like me, just here to watch. Not all that many of them are actually holding mousetraps, you'll notice."

"Enough," said Billy.

A teacher with a clipboard stood at the starting line. A man with a pencil over his ear was nearby with a shiny metal measuring tape to measure the distance each mousetrap car went.

Billy got in line behind a hefty guy with freckled ears. The guy turned around and stared at Billy's mousetrap.

"Don't pay any attention to him," Paul whispered. "He's just trying to psych you out."

"Yeah, well, it's working," muttered Billy.

A mousetrap car with huge wheels made out of phonograph records was the first one at the starting position. Its wheels were so large that Paul couldn't see the mousetrap at all. Paul and Billy exchanged a glance. Wheels so big would be sure to carry the mousetrap a long way.

"I wish we'd thought of that," said Paul.

"I tried it," the boy with the freckled ears said. "It doesn't work because the phonograph records add more weight. That's why you can't get any advantage that way."

Paul and Billy fell silent. The boy with the freckled ears seemed to know everything. Paul hadn't even thought about the weight of the wheels slowing down the car.

The car's phonograph record wheels began turning, and Paul and Billy watched breathlessly as it wobbled forward. Suddenly one of the phonograph records came loose and landed with a clatter on the polished wood of the gym floor.

The boy with the freckled ears guffawed. In Paul's opinion the guy with the freckled ears made Tiffany look like a recent graduate from charm school.

One by one kids went up to the starting tape and set off their mousetrap vehicles. Some of the other cars did not go far at all. Paul began to feel hopeful that Billy's entry might have a chance. At last the boy with the freckled ears knelt at the starting tape with his mousetrap. His car looked like Billy's, but it seemed to Paul that the rubber band looked fatter. He tapped lightly on his trap. It shot off and rolled down the gym floor. Paul and Billy looked at each other in dismay. The mousetrap had gone farther than any of the others. The man with the metal measuring tape had to back away to measure the distance. The boy with freckled ears smiled broadly. "Pretty good," he said. "Pret-ty darn good, if I do say so myself."

"Okay, Billy." Paul nudged his friend. "You're next."

Billy gave his name and his school to the lady

with the clipboard, then set his mousetrap car down on the gym floor. Kneeling beside it, he took a deep breath and tapped it with his pencil. The mousetrap went off with a snap, and the car began to roll. It went a good distance, but Paul could tell it did not go quite as far as the freckled boy's car. The man with the measuring tape had to step forward to measure it.

"It's okay," Paul told Billy. "Remember our team gets points even if you place second or third."

Billy looked crestfallen. "I wonder what made his go so far?"

"Hot air," said Paul scornfully. "Look, now that you're through, let's run over to the art building and see how Carlos is getting along."

The boys rushed to the art building. Paul was enjoying himself. Kids hurried everywhere, stray photocopied schedules littered the ground, and excitement was in the air. Paul hadn't realized science could be so much fun. He loved being able to go all over the campus without anybody saying "Wait a minute" or "Watch out."

"Here it is," said Billy. "The art building."

"I know that," said Paul. "I know where everything is around here, remember? This is where my dad works."

When Paul and Billy stepped inside the art building, they came upon a scene of noise and confusion. Near the entrance a lady sat at a card table that was stacked with papers. "What is the immature form of the frog?" she barked.

"Tadpole," panted a short kid in a green T-shirt.

"Correct," she said crisply. The kid ran at once to the next card table, and a second kid skidded to a stop beside the lady, his mouth open expectantly. "How often do we have a full moon?" the lady asked.

"Gee, I don't know." His face fell.

"Incorrect," she said, making a check mark on her paper.

Paul looked around. "Do you see Carlos anywhere?" he asked Billy.

Billy pointed. "Down there."

Carlos was at the other end of the hall. Paul and Billy watched him amble to a card table. "Good grief," said Paul in disgust. "You'd think he'd at least get a move on. Let's go hurry him up some."

The lady at the card table peered at Paul over her glasses. "No one is allowed to speak to the contestants," she said.

"I give up," Paul said. "Carlos is a goner. I don't even want to watch. Let's go check out what Suzy and Kate are doing."

As they left the art building, Tiffany called to them. "Hey, Paul! Hey, Billy! Has anybody on your team won anything yet?"

"We're not sure," said Paul.

"Somebody from our team won the mousetrap race," Tiffany said proudly.

"Freckled ears?" asked Paul.

"Yeah. That's him. Curtis Bland. I might win first place with my egg protector, too," said Tiffany. "So far we're doing just great."

Paul had left his egg protector in Mrs. Melenik's van because he didn't want to carry it around with him. Suddenly he had an awful thought. What if Mrs. Melenik had locked the van when she went off?

"What time is it?" Paul asked Billy.

"It's almost quarter of ten. I guess we'd better not look for Suzy and Kate. It's just about time for your egg drop."

"I've got to go get my egg protector," said Paul. "You come with me."

"You better hurry," said Tiffany. "You might miss the event."

Paul gritted his teeth. "We won't miss it," he said.

Billy and Paul ran to the parking lot. Paul tugged on the door of the van. "Locked!" he cried. "Try the other door, Billy."

"It's locked, too!" Billy yelled.

"There must be some way we can break into this thing," Paul said. He looked around for a brick or a rock. With a sinking feeling in his stomach, he wondered what his mother would say if he broke the window to Mrs. Melenik's van. He would be grounded for the rest of his life probably. It was even possible he could get locked up in jail for doing something like that. He wished he knew for sure if people in the fourth grade ever got put in jail. But he *had* to get his egg protector somehow or another.

"We've got to find Mrs. Melenik and get the key," said Billy.

"Right!" Paul exclaimed, relieved. They needed to find Mrs. Melenik! He should have thought of that. "Let's split up," he said. "That way we can cover more ground."

Billy went off to check the art building, and Paul went in the other direction. Air burned his throat as he ran full speed to the gym. Paul burst into the gym and looked around. The event called metric estimation was in progress, but there was no sign of Mrs. Melenik. Where could she be? He felt almost dizzy with anxiety as his eyes darted back and forth searching desperately for her. He couldn't miss the egg drop. He just *couldn't*. He ran blindly out of the gym.

"Hey, Paul!" Billy waved with both arms. "I found her. She's unlocking the van now."

Paul's feeling of relief was so great that he felt his knees buckle. "Great!" he yelled.

"We can make it!" said Billy. "Don't worry."

When Paul reached the parking lot, Mrs. Melenik was standing by the van. "Cutting it a bit close, aren't you, Paul?" She smiled. "You'd better hurry on over to the ball field now."

Paul took the egg protector from her, cradling it carefully in his hands. The grade A egg was already in it, nestled in several layers of bubble wrap that had been carefully stapled in place. He was sure it was secure; he was *sure* that egg wouldn't break. Just the same, he didn't want to drop it until he got to the playing field.

Billy ran up to him. "We can make it," he said. "You've got three whole minutes."

The two boys hurried toward the baseball diamond at the south edge of the campus. When they got there, Paul spotted Tiffany sitting on the top row of the bleachers.

"Mine won't break," Paul said in a low voice. He hoped he was right about that.

"Have you tried dropping it off a bleacher already?" Billy asked, impressed.

"Well, not a bleacher exactly, but a ladder. That's almost as good. And it worked okay then."

"A ladder's pretty tall," agreed Billy. He hesitated. "Was it a tall ladder, Paul?"

"Not especially," said Paul. His stomach squeezed with nervousness. "But this is a good egg protector. Believe me, Billy, you don't get an egg any more protected than this."

The boys took a seat on the bottom row of the bleachers because Paul wanted to get as far away from Tiffany as possible. Paul's father came up to the bleachers wearing his favorite floppy cotton hat.

"Boys and girls," Mr. Fenner called, "I'd like you to bring your egg protectors down for registration. Since you'll be handing your egg protectors over to us for testing, we have to make sure which person each egg belongs to."

"You don't get to drop them off the bleachers yourself?" Billy asked Paul.

"My dad's probably afraid we'd be so dumb we'd fall off the bleachers if we tried it."

Paul went up in his turn to get a round sticker that said "eight." He noticed that Tiffany had managed to get a sticker that said "one." Boy, that was just like her, he thought. She *would* get number one.

Paul gave his egg protector to a tall skinny man in an official's hat.

"Is your egg inside that hat, Paul?" Tiffany asked.

"Yeah." He sneaked a look at Tiffany's egg protector. It was plenty colorful, but it did not look too sturdy. The egg was surrounded by bent red and yellow striped straws.

Tiffany gave hers to the man in the hat. "Be careful with it," she warned him.

The man placed Tiffany's egg protector in the basket beside Paul's.

"I thought they were going to let us drop them off the bleachers ourselves," said Tiffany, frowning.

"It's better this way," said Paul, "because we can stand down on the ground and see whether the eggs break or not."

"Hey, that's right!" Billy brightened. "Let's go around to the back of the bleachers, where we can get a good view."

"Has your team won any ribbons yet?" asked Tiffany.

"You just asked me that a minute ago," said Paul. "I already told you that I don't know."

Suzy and Kate ran up to them, their cheeks pink. "We got a second place," Suzy said breathlessly.

"We couldn't tell which was the baking soda and which was the plaster of Paris," Kate said.

"Maybe you should have practiced more," said Paul severely.

"It was hard," said Suzy. "There were a lot of things to identify, and they mostly looked alike. Second place isn't bad." The girls smiled happily at each other.

"Stand back, kids!" a man yelled.

The children quickly stepped away from the

bleachers. Large pieces of plywood had been laid on the ground behind the bleachers to form a crash pad for the egg protectors.

Tiffany did not go first after all because it turned out the numbers were being drawn out of a hat. "Number five," someone called. A brown cardboard package fell to the ground, and almost right away a sticky yellow egg yolk leaked from it. A woman with a clipboard picked up the egg package gingerly, made a note, and placed it in a cardboard box.

"Boy, this is going to be messy," said Paul. "All those broken eggs." He folded his arms, trying to ignore his racing heart. "I bet mine's the only one that's not going to break."

"Number twelve," called the man.

Number twelve hit with a splat.

"Oh, no!" A boy near Paul slapped his hand to his forehead. "That was mine."

"Number one!"

Tiffany looked up.

In a colorful blur her package of straws fell to the ground. The egg broke.

"Oh, no," said Tiffany. Her face turned pink. "I told my dad we should have kept looking till we found paper straws. It's those cheap plastic straws from McDonald's that ruined everything. They were too slippery, and they slipped out of place, that was the trouble. We should have bought paper straws."

Paul did his best not to smile. He did not want to be nasty about winning, like the boy with the freckled ears. But after all the times Tiffany had told him that she was going to win, the crunching sound of her egg breaking had been music to his ears.

The woman collected Tiffany's broken egg and the straws and added them to the cardboard box.

"Why are they picking up the broken ones?" asked Billy. "I mean, if they're broken we know they've lost, right? I don't get it."

"But if they *all* broke," said Paul, "then they'd have to weigh them. Remember, the ties are broken by weight." In Paul's private opinion they could have saved themselves the trouble of collecting all those egg packages. He was pretty sure that his egg wasn't going to break.

The children watched as one egg after another broke against the plywood.

"I bet they're all going to break," said Tiffany. "It's because of the way they're dropping them. I bet it wouldn't have happened if they'd let us drop our own. That guy is probably throwing them down as hard as he can. He just wants everybody to lose, that's all. This is such a dumb contest. Don't you think they're all going to break?"

Paul didn't answer. He was sure, absolutely

86

sure, that his was not going to break. But he was almost afraid to breathe until he had seen it with his own eyes.

"Num-ber eight!"

Paul stiffened. This one was his. The blue party hat somersaulted off the back of the bleacher and landed on the plywood. It rolled around in a semi-circle and then lay there. His egg had not broken. Paul exhaled.

Billy grabbed his sleeve. "Way to go, man. It didn't break!"

"Maybe it cracked," said Tiffany hopefully.

The woman picked up Paul's egg protector with a smile. She looked at it curiously, then added it to the cardboard box.

"Man!" Paul sagged against Billy. "For a minute there I was really worried. I tested it, sure, but I never actually dropped it off a bleacher." He looked around. "I wonder when they're going to announce the winner."

"They've still got some eggs left," Billy pointed out. "I guess that's why they can't announce it yet. They could have a tie."

"Congratulations, Paul," said Suzy. "That was really good. You might even be the only one on our team to win a first place."

Paul felt himself grow warm with pride. "I'm going to go ask Dad when they're going to announce it." He ran around to the front of the bleachers and found his father talking to another professor.

"Dad!" said Paul, horrified. "You missed it!"

Mr. Fenner started. "Did I, Paul? Gee, I'm sorry. Gene and I just got involved in talking, and I guess I forgot to look."

"I can't believe you missed the whole thing!" said Paul.

"I thought they were still at it," said Mr. Fenner guiltily.

"Yeah, but mine and Tiffany's have already dropped, and that was the important part."

"How'd it go?"

"Tiffany's busted," Paul reported with satisfaction. "But mine didn't have a scratch. When are they going to announce who got first place? I just want to see Tiffany's face when I get my ribbon."

Mr. Fenner glanced at his watch. "Well, let's see. The awards ceremony is in forty-five minutes."

"Not until then?"

Mr. Fenner smiled. "They can't announce anything officially just yet, Paul."

"Suzy and Kate said they got second place in their event, so they must have announced that."

"Not officially. You see, they have to examine every entry and make sure it followed the rules. They have to weigh things in cases where the ties are broken by weight, and so forth."

Paul's dad pulled some change out of his pocket. "Why don't you and Billy go get yourselves a snack. It'll be time for the awards ceremony before you know it."

Reluctantly Paul went to get Billy, and they went together to find the snack machines.

"Boy, you did great, Paul," said Billy. "Yours was the only one that didn't break. You should have stayed and watched the rest of them. Yours was the best, no question about that."

"It wasn't bad," said Paul modestly. He felt light-headed with relief and pleasure.

As they passed the art building, they met Carlos. "Carlos, old buddy," said Paul, grinning. "How's it going?"

"Paul won the egg drop," said Billy. "His was the only one that didn't break."

"So how'd you do in yours?" asked Paul.

"Dunno," said Carlos cheerfully. "I guess we'll find out at the awards ceremony."

"You must have *some* idea," said Paul. "Who finished first?"

"It's not easy to figure out, Paul," said Carlos. "It's not like a race. They write down the time when you start and when you finish. But since you don't know when everybody else started, you don't really know who went fastest."

"You couldn't tell at all?" Paul was disappointed.

89

With him taking a first place and Suzy and Kate and Billy getting seconds, he was beginning to think their team had a chance at least of placing, maybe. If only Carlos had a little more on the ball, he could have been more certain of it.

"Everything was all confused—people running around and everything," said Carlos. "Besides, the time it takes you is only one part of it. The other thing is how many questions you got right."

"So, did you get a lot of questions right?" asked Paul.

"I guess."

Paul brightened.

"I got a lot wrong, too, though," said Carlos thoughtfully.

"Figures," Paul muttered.

"We're going to go get something to eat," said Billy. "Want to come?"

"Nah," said Carlos. "I'm going to walk around some."

"He's probably going to look at clouds," said Paul darkly.

Chapter
Ten

When time came for the awards ceremony, Paul and Billy filed into the auditorium seats near Mrs. Melenik.

"I'm glad I caught you, Paul," Mrs. Melenik whispered. "There's been a problem with your entry in the egg drop."

Paul's stomach felt as if he were falling down an elevator shaft. "How can there be a problem?" he whispered. His voice seemed to be giving out. "I don't get it."

"Well, dear, you remember the rule that no metal could be used in the egg protector?"

"Yeah, but I used paper and bubble wrap. Bubble wrap is just plastic. I didn't make it out of metal!"

Mrs. Melenik watched him sympathetically. "There was the little matter of the staples."

"The staples!" Paul fell into a folding seat, stunned.

"It's the rule," Mrs. Melenik said regretfully. "I didn't notice the staples myself, dear. I'm so sorry."

Billy's mouth was hanging open. "Does this mean Paul's egg protector doesn't win?"

"Unhappily," said Mrs. Melenik, "Paul's entry has been disqualified."

Paul found himself unable to speak for some minutes. After flashing Paul a sympathetic smile, Mrs. Melenik moved away. Paul croaked, "It's not fair."

"Golly, just because of those dumb staples," said Billy. "That's awful."

Tiffany sat down in the row in front of them. "Hi, Paul," she said. "Has your team won anything yet?"

"Paul's egg package got disqualified because it had staples!" Billy burst out.

Paul hit him with his elbow. "You didn't have to tell her that."

"Gee, that's too bad," said Tiffany. "I know just how you feel, Paul. If my dad had gotten the right kind of straws, mine would have worked just right. I mean, I had a good idea. And light? It was the *lightest*. It hardly weighed *anything*. The only problem with it was that we used the wrong kind of straws."

Paul folded his arms and remained silent.

"He's not too happy," Billy said in a stage whisper. "On account of those staples."

Mr. Fenner came over to them. "Hi, guys. How's it going?"

"Dad, they've disqualified my entry!" Paul felt like bursting into tears.

"It was the staples," Billy put in breathlessly. "You weren't supposed to use metal, but Paul forgot about the staples."

Mr. Fenner's eyes were sympathetic. "Oh, Paul. I'm sorry. I didn't think about the staples myself."

"It's not fair!" Paul cried. "A few staples isn't the same as using metal."

"Staples *are* made out of metal," said Billy.

Paul turned on him. "It's not the same thing!" he said loudly. "It's not fair!"

His dad squeezed his shoulder. "It's tough, Paul. I know it is, but try to be a good sport. And after all, we're all out here having fun together. That's the important thing, isn't it?"

Paul gave his father a black look. If he had won, then that would have been fun. This was not fun.

Paul felt sick. He couldn't believe this had happened to him. A minute ago he was a winner. Now his victory had been snatched from him. And yet his was the *only* egg that hadn't broken. It was so unfair.

Onstage a plump woman tapped on the microphone. "Testing, testing." Mr. Fenner sat down behind the boys.

"Welcome," said the woman, "to our first annual Science Olympiad. I am Mrs. Baker and I am here to present awards to a lot of hardworking boys and girls."

The auditorium burst into applause. Mrs. Baker went on to make a few remarks about the importance of science in the modern world, then began presenting the ribbons. "In the egg drop—first place goes to Tiffany Bonner."

Tiffany jumped up. "Aw-right!" she exclaimed.

Paul stared at the back of the seat ahead of him so hard that if he had had X-ray vision, it would have burst into flames.

The second- and third-place winners were called up to the stage in their turn. Tiffany came back to her seat, holding a blue ribbon. After she sat down, she promptly twisted around to face Paul and Billy. She was beaming. "I got a blue ribbon. Want to see it?"

"Not especially," said Paul.

"That's nice, Tiffany," said Billy.

Paul didn't see why Billy had to go out of his way to be pleasant to Tiffany.

"And now," said Mrs. Baker, "for the mousetrap car. First place goes to Curtis Bland."

The boy with the freckled ears strutted up to

the stage. "Second place," Mrs. Bland went on, "goes to Billy Blakely."

"Hey," said Billy, jumping up from his seat. "Second place is pretty good."

The awful unfairness of it hit Paul like a blow. The best egg protector, his own, had been unfairly disqualified on a very minor technicality. But Billy hadn't even built his mousetrap car, and it had won second place. If anything was going to be disqualified, it should have been Billy's car.

Paul couldn't believe it! He had actually persuaded his mom and dad to come up with this idea for a Science Olympiad. It had been all because of him that it had happened in the first place. All the people with their clipboards and their silly little entries, and their questions and answers—it was all because of him. If he had kept his mouth shut about the homework, he wouldn't be sitting here being miserable right this minute.

Absorbed as he was in his own unhappiness, Paul only dimly noticed that Suzy and Kate took second place in the detect-a-substance event and that Carlos took second place in the decathlon.

"How about that!" said Billy. "We've got three second places! That's not so bad."

"I bet Carlos just about fainted," said Paul sourly.

"He must have gotten a lot of the questions right," said Billy. "He's pretty smart."

"Carlos?" said Paul incredulously.

"Yeah. He knows a lot of stuff. You ought to talk to him sometime."

A girl who looked vaguely familiar to Paul took a third place in metric estimation. "That's Angela," said Billy. "She's in Mrs. Green's class." And Robbie Hinton, also in Mrs. Green's class, took a second place in ocean life.

"What's wrong with first place?" Paul asked. "How come nobody in our school ever gets first place?" He was careful not to say this loudly enough for Tiffany to hear.

"You would have gotten first place if it hadn't been for the staples," said Billy loyally.

It was true. But it didn't do them a bit of good. Paul wondered how many points Tiffany's team had. He had seen that Tiffany had gotten first place and Curtis had gotten a first, but he didn't know how the rest of the team had done because they were announcing kids names only, not their schools.

The microphone rang so loudly it hurt Paul's ears, and Mrs. Baker had to jiggle it until it stopped. "And now," she said, "the prizes for the best teams. These are the teams that got the most number of points overall. First place goes to Fuller Elementary."

"That's us!" cried Billy. "We won!"

"What?" For a moment Paul felt dazed.

"Boy," said Tiffany respectfully, "all those second places must have added up."

"Yay!" yelled Suzy and Kate. They jumped up and down in their seats. Suzy stood up and waved at Paul and Billy.

"I don't care," said Tiffany, "because I got first place for my egg protector."

"Second place goes to Willowford Elementary."

"That's us," said Tiffany. "Second place is pretty good."

"First place is better." Paul looked around for his father, but he didn't see him. Paul was disappointed. He hoped his dad hadn't left the auditorium before the good part.

"We'll probably get first place next year," said Tiffany.

Mrs. Baker announced the third-place winner, then concluded, "I want to congratulate all you boys and girls on your effort and to thank everyone for all the work that went into making this Science Olympiad such a success. Thank you."

"Number one!" shrieked Suzy, running over to Paul and Billy. "We won!"

"I thought for sure Willowford was going to win," said Billy. "They had two first places."

"Yeah," said Suzy, "they did have two firsts, but I don't think any of the rest of their entries even placed."

"Slow and steady wins the race," said Carlos.

Carlos would say something like that, thought Paul.

Carlos frowned. "Tough luck about those staples, Paul."

Paul hunched his shoulders and looked down. He guessed everybody in the county knew about the staples by now. "Yeah," he said. "Well, those things happen, I guess."

Mrs. Melenik began herding the kids together.

Mr. Fenner found Paul and patted him on the back. "I'll meet you at home, Paul."

"Why don't I just go home with you?" said Paul. "And Billy, too. Then we could go by for pizza."

Mr. Fenner grinned. "And miss the celebration? Nah, you'll want to ride back with your team."

"We're number one!" screamed Suzy.

Paul looked at her in astonishment. He had never heard Suzy scream before. Mrs. Melenik covered her ears. "That's enough, boys and girls."

"Num-ber one!" chanted Suzy and Kate in unison.

The boys quickly joined in. "Num-ber one! Num-ber one!" The kids linked arms and staggered out to Mrs. Melenik's van. Taped to the size of the van was a piece of poster board that said "Fuller Elementary—#1."

Paul flushed with pleasure. His dad must have run back to his office and made the poster. That was why he had gone away for a minute.

Paul spotted Tiffany climbing into a van farther down the parking lot. Billy and Suzy waved at her. "We're num-ber one! We're num-ber one!" the kids chanted. After a minute Paul joined in. "Number one!" he screamed. He yelled so loud that his throat hurt, but it felt good.

"Wait till next year, suckers!" Curtis yelled.

"Num-ber one!" chanted the Fuller kids.

Paul got in the van and leaned back in his seat. Okay, so he had missed out on the egg drop. The important thing was that his team had won. He guessed that would show Tiffany a thing or two about who had the best school. *That* ought to shut her up.

"Hey," said Billy, "you aren't yelling!" He poked Paul with his elbow.

Paul laughed. "Num-ber one!" they screamed together.

Chapter
Eleven

Monday afternoon at the YMCA, Paul shook the water out of his ears and settled down on the couch with his homework. He liked to work with the sound of Ranger Bob's cartoon show in the background. He was, of course, too old to be seriously interested in cartoons, but he liked to glance up occasionally just to see what was going on. There was something comforting about the world of cartoons. Every day the characters got flattened by steamrollers only to bounce back fully inflated. If electric shocks made a cartoon cat's hair stand on end, a second later he was back chasing the canary with new energy. Paul gave a contented sigh as he confronted the heading on his sheet of notebook paper. "Vermont," it said. It was a good beginning. But if the materials he had sent off for from the state of Vermont didn't come soon, he was going to have a problem.

"Hey, Paul!" Paul winced as Tiffany plopped down on the couch next to him. "You watching cartoons?"

"I work better when the television's on, that's all," said Paul. "I'm not really watching."

"I like cartoons, too," said Tiffany. She craned her neck to read his paper. " 'Vermont.' Hey, my class is doing state projects, too. Is that your state? My state is Idaho."

Paul was so relieved that Tiffany had not picked Vermont, too, that he smiled.

On the television screen a window closed in the cartoon cat's face, and the canary flew away. "Duh!" said the cat stupidly. The picture faded away. Paul stared at the screen, thinking that life was more like a cartoon than he had ever thought. He had been flattened when his egg protector was disqualified. The unfairness of it still burned whenever he thought of it. It had been like being run over by a steamroller. And yet he had bounced back. His team had won. And that was the important thing.

"And now, boys and girls," said Ranger Bob, "let's look at some of the pictures you have sent me. Here's a picture of a . . . let me see, I believe it's a dragon, from Paul Fenner."

"It's a sea serpent, for pete's sake!" Paul exclaimed. "Can't you recognize a sea serpent?"

He couldn't believe it! His picture was on TV!

"I like those bright colors," said Ranger Bob. "That's a very impressive dragon. Yes, sirree. And now here's a mermaid from Tiffany Bonner. Very pretty."

"Paul, we're on TV!" Tiffany grabbed Paul's sleeve.

"Shut up!" Paul hissed. He didn't want to miss anything.

"You know, boys and girls," said Ranger Bob, "I think that Paul and Tiffany must be friends. You see how much their pictures are alike?"

The cameraman panned from Tiffany's drawing back to Paul's so the viewers could see the resemblance. Tiffany's was clearly labeled "MERMAID" in red crayon.

"Well, good grief," said Paul indignantly. "They only look alike because she copied mine." But, of course, Ranger Bob couldn't hear him.

"I think," said Ranger Bob, "that they must have worked on these pictures together. And now here's a very nice picture of a house from Randy Simmons in Charlotte."

But Paul didn't hear any more. Friends! he thought, stunned. Right there on television, Ranger Bob had called him and Tiffany friends.

Tiffany bounced up and down on the couch.

"How about that? He showed our pictures! Isn't that totally neat? I wish my mother were here. I wish she had seen it."

"Well, you don't have to go around bragging about it to everybody," said Paul.

"I'm not bragging. I was just pointing out that Ranger Bob showed my picture. That is *not* bragging."

"Well, you don't have to point it out to me, Tiffany," said Paul, "because I already noticed it."

Tiffany was silent for a moment, so silent it made Paul nervous. When she got as quiet as that, he found he couldn't even concentrate on cartoons, much less on his Vermont report.

"Did you ever see my blue ribbon, Paul?" she said at last. "I brought it with me today so I could show Mrs. Horowitz." She laid the blue ribbon on her knee. Paul was surprised to see that she looked a little sad. He didn't know what she had to be sad about. She had won, hadn't she? But his heart squeezed inside him, and to his amazement he heard himself saying, "It's real nice, Tiff."

She smiled up at him. "Yeah, it is, isn't it? I never got a blue ribbon before. Mrs. Horowitz says, though, that if I work hard I'll get lots of blue ribbons in swimming."

I'm not going to hold my breath, thought Paul, who remembered how she had looked flailing around in the water not all that long ago. It gave him a lot of satisfaction to think that Tiffany was still only a beginner in swimming. He didn't say that, though. And heck, if it was such a big deal for her, he was glad she got the silly blue ribbon at the contest.

A horn honked and Paul looked up to see his father's car poised at the curb just beyond the glass doors. He jumped up. "Bye," he said. "See you tomorrow."

Paul was surprised at himself. He had actually been almost friendly to Tiffany. He didn't even mind that much anymore that Ranger Bob had said that he and Tiffany were friends.

Paul ran out to the car and jumped in.

"Hiya, sport," said Mr. Fenner. "Did you have a good day?"

Paul smiled. "Okay."

Tiffany pressed her nose against the glass door and waved at them. Mr. Fenner waved back, then drove away.

"Is Tiffany still bugging you?" Mr. Fenner lifted his eyebrows questioningly.

"Nah." Paul leaned his head back against the seat and let a smile grow slowly on his face. "I don't let her get to me. Not now that we both know whose team is number one."

About the Author

JANICE HARRELL decided she wanted to be a writer when she was in the fourth grade. She grew up in Florida and received her master's and doctorate degrees in eighteenth-century English literature from the University of Florida. After teaching college English for a number of years, she began to write full time.

She lives in Rocky Mount, North Carolina, with her husband, a psychologist, and their daughter. Ms. Harrell is a compulsive traveler—some of the countries she has visited are Greece, France, Egypt, Italy, England, and Spain—and she loves taking photographs.

Read these exciting adventures from Minstrel® Books:

Monica and Dee Ellen have pledged their friendship in ketchup instead of in blood! Together they solve mysteries in *The Ketchup Sisters* by Judith Hollands

•

Ernie learns *How to Survive Third Grade* with the help of a new friend. By Laurie Lawlor

•

All Bertine wanted was a bear. But suddenly she had ten walking, talking Teddies that sprouted from *The Teddy Bear Tree*. By Barbara Dillon

•

Liza's in trouble before class even begins! She thinks *Third Grade is Terrible*. By Barbara Baker

•

Who has the cooties in second grade? *Itchy Richard*, by Jamie Gilson

•

Meet Mr. Pin, the penguin detective who can't stay out of trouble: *The Mysterious Cases of Mr. Pin* and *Mr. Pin: The Chocolate Files*, by Mary Elise Monsell

These titles and many more fun books are available from

MINSTREL® BOOKS

Published by Pocket Books

548D-01